Ministero per i Ben'
Soprintendenza spe

C000298776

·the·batns· ·of·caracalla· guide

Electa

Editorial Coordination
Cristina Garbagna

Editing
Gail Swerling

Graphic Coordination
Angelo Galiotto

Graphic Design
Tassinari/Vetta Leonardo Sonnoli
with Alessandro Panichi

Page Layout
Claudia Brambilla

Technical Coordination
Lara Panigas

Quality Control
Giancarlo Berti

Translation
Sandra Ciuffini
Richard Sadleir

Texts by
Marina Piranomonte

Reprint 2014
First edition 2008

An editorial production by Mondadori Electa, S.p.A., Milan

www.electaweb.com

Contents

1

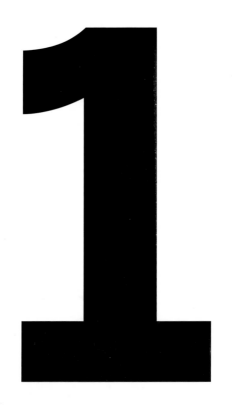

The History of the Site

The History of the Site

The Baths of Caracalla are one of the largest and best preserved thermal complexes of antiquity. Because of their remarkable height, exceeding 30 meters in many parts, the extensive remains of the Baths (or *thermae*) provide a glimpse of the magnificence of the thermal complex, second in size only to the Baths of Diocletian dated almost a century later. We can only imagine its splendor looking at the dimension of the structure and the monumentality of its rooms. Two upper stories and two underground levels of the complex still stand.

The Baths were probably commissioned by Septimius Severus and inaugurated in AD 216 under the reign of his son Marcus Aurelius Antoninus Bassianus, known as Caracalla. They were built in the southern part of the city, in Regio XII, the *Piscina Publica* (public bath). This area was beautified and monumentalized by the Severan dynasty, with the construction of the *via Nova,* leading to the new baths commissioned by Caracalla and the *Septizodium,* a grandiose multilevel nymphaeum similar to a stage set from a Hellenistic theater, which was built by Septimius Severus on the southwestern slopes of the Palatine hill, as a monumental backdrop to the beginning of *via Appia*.

Elio Sparziano, in his work *The Life of Caracalla*, narrates that the Emperor built the "thermas eximias et magnificentissimas" (noble and magnificent baths), but we know from other sources that they were completed with porticos and additional decorations by his successors Heliogabalus and Alexander. The Baths were probably finished in AD 235 Restorations were undertaken by Aurelian after a fire and by Diocletian

The *caldarium*

who worked on the aqueduct (*aqua Antoniniana*) which took from him the name of *forma Iobia* (of Jupiter). Constantine modified the *caldarium* with the insertion of a semi-circular apse, leaving evidence of his work in an inscription preserved in the underground level of the complex. The Baths were perfectly functional in the fifth century AD Polemon Silvius refers to the Baths as one of the seven wonders of Rome, famous for the richness of decoration and for the artworks adorning them. Olympiodorus speaks of their grandeur which can be measured also by the 1600 "seats" available for those visiting. This last interpretation remains unclear: reference is probably made to the number of bathers visiting at one time, since the one of bathers per day was calculated to be between 6000 and 8000. That the Baths were perfectly functional in that period is also demonstrated by the data gathered during very recent excavations in the galleries, that show evidence of the type of work done in those years.

The Baths of Caracalla were in use for only three centuries. They were completely abandoned soon after the siege of Rome in the year AD 537, by Vitige, the King of the Goths, who severed the aqueducts with the intention of cutting the water sup-

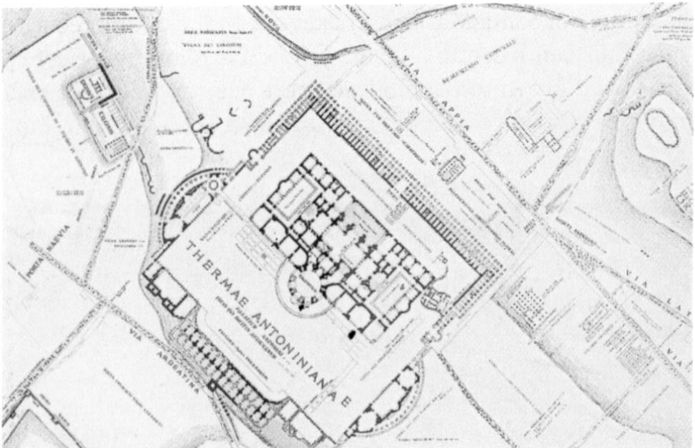

The Baths of Caracalla in the *Forma Urbis Romae* by Rodolfo Lanciani (1893–1901)

ply to Rome. From that moment, the Baths lost their importance: their geographical position was too far from the center where the population, fearing the invaders, was gathering. Years of abandon followed during which the monument was most probably used as a cemetery for pilgrims who fell ill during their voyage to Rome and were sheltered in the nearby *Xenodochium* of Saint Nereo and Saint Achilleo. This has been confirmed in recent years by the uncovering of a few humble tombs of the sixth–seventh century inside the surrounding walls. There is some evidence in the *Liber Pontificalis* (Pontifical Book) of restorations done to the aqueduct dating up to the ninth century by Pope Adrianus I, Sergius II and Nicolaus I. Traces of limestone deposits removed from the pipe places, together with other deposits found in the galleries, confirm that water still continued to flow freely for centuries. As early as the twelfth century the Baths of Caracalla were used as a quarry for material used in the decoration of churches and palaces. Three capitals with eagles and lightning bolts, symbols of Jupiter, from the eastern side *palaestra* (gym), were installed, after suitable adjustments, in the Cathedral of Pisa. Eight capitals, representing Isis, Serapi and Harpocrates (Egyptian gods), were removed from the libraries and placed in the Church of Santa Maria in Trastevere. In the notary records of the fourteenth century, the Baths of Caracalla were referred to as "palatium Antonianum" and were used as vineyards and gardens due to the availability of large quantities of water. But,

Inscription relating to a restoration
by Constantine, preserved
in the underground levels

even in the fifteenth century the impressive ruins of the Baths evoked enthusiasm from the few visitors, one of whom was Poggio Fiorentino, who wrote in 1450: "Many ruins remain of the Baths of Antoninus, the son of Severus, more than the others, and they receive high praises from onlookers, who cannot imagine the function of such a massive and marvelous structure, with its array of immense columns notable for both their size and the variety of marbles used in them."

During the papacy of Julius II in the first half of the sixteenth century, many columns were still standing even though they were covered by ruins. Even the central body of the Baths could still be visited. A few years later, the site deteriorated significantly due to the excavations carried out by Pope Paul III Farnese for the construction of his new palazzo. The Pope's excavations were a fundamental moment for the history of the Baths. In fact, between 1545 and 1547 large statues, precious objects, bronzes and colossal marble groups were unearthed, creating great interest at the time. After the Farnese excavations, the Baths of Caracalla fell into a long period of oblivion. In the second half of the sixteenth century, Pope Paul V granted conveyance of the Baths to the Jesuits of the

Detail of the fresco portraying the head of Anubis, in the house dating back to the Hadrianic period located under the Baths

A wall of the *lararium*, which originated from the house dating back to the Hadrianic period under the Baths, now placed in a room of the eastern *palaestra*

Roman Seminary and they were utilized as a playground for children. It is believed that even Saint Filippo Neri would bring the children of his Oratory to the Baths and that it was he who commissioned the fresco of the *Madonna Supported by an Angel,* still visible in the area overlooking the *natatio.* Between the sixteenth and eighteenth century, interest in the grandiose architecture of the building was renewed, and well-known designs were produced by famous artists, such as Falda, Giuliano da Sangallo, Palladio, Nolli.

In 1824, Count Egidio Di Velo carried out systematic excavations in the central body of the building, uncovering, among other things, the famous mosaic floors depicting athletes. These floors are now preserved in the Vatican museums. Excavations were then conducted by Canina in the *frigidarium* till the middle of the century and then by Guidi between 1860 and 1867. The latter uncovered in the southeastern corner of the Baths, at 8 meters below the existing walking level, a rich *domus* (home) of the Hadrianic period with mosaic floors and frescos of the second style on the walls. The frescos found in the most interesting

Fresco depicting the Madonna supported by an Angel, preserved in one of the passage areas between the *natatio* and the *frigidarium*

Statue of Artemis from the Baths
of Caracalla (found in 1996).
Rome, Museo Nazionale Romano,
Octagonal Hall of the Baths of Diocletian

room, the *lararium*, were separated from the walls and restored in 1975, and they are displayed in an area of the eastern *palaestra*. Between 1866 and 1869, restoration in the central body of the building uncovered the famous capitals bearing figures, the columns of porphyry and the torso of Hercules. In 1870, when the monument became property of the Italian government, further excavations were made by Pietro Rosa in the eastern *palaestra*. It was only during 1878 and 1879, that Fiorelli uncovered, in the *caldarium*, a marble floor in *opus sectile* (ornamental motif) and a mosaic floor in the western *palaestra* which was completely unearthed.

At the beginning of the twentieth century, the surrounding walls and part of the underground levels were explored. These excavations uncovered a number of rooms within the large western exedra, the library and, in the underground, the *Mythraeum* (temple in honor of god Mithra) and what was recently identified as a water mill. The systematic exploration of the galleries, in part carried out during the eighteenth and nineteenth centuries, started in 1901 and continued on the eastern side in 1938 and 1939, in occasion of the installation of the stage of the Opera Theater in the *caldarium*. Restorations were executed by the Governorship with the assistance of the Superintendent of the Monuments in Lazio. No documentation, unfortunately, exists to this effect except for a few vivacious sketches. After this period, the most important archeological excavations in the Baths were those of the 1980s, which revealed and reconstituted the ancient plan of the Baths by clearing away the thick vegetation and illegal houses which had covered the building, and restoring the southern wall with the cisterns, the southwestern library, and the so called Temple of Jupiter on the eastern side. A significant moment for the Baths in the 1990s was 1993, year of the last Summer lyrical season of the Opera Theater in the *caldarium*, after it had been occupied since 1938.

Finally, in 1996, the last statuary was discovered by the author of this book, while installing electrical cables for the new lighting system. The headless statue of Artemis, standing and dressed in a short chiton, was used as a base for the road in the underground galleries during a restoration of the fifth century. As of April 1997, this statue and many others from the Baths of Caracalla can be found in the Octagonal Hall (*Aula Ottagona*) of the Baths of Diocletian.

In 1998 a careful and attentive project liberated the Baths from all the rusty structures of the old stage of the Opera House, which dated from 1937.

The work lasted about a year and was followed by preparations for the Holy Year, with the construction of the new facilities for the public and a new outer fence.

In 2001 the Baths were reopened to the accompaniment of classical music: for two years they were used to house the summer seasons of the opera and the Accademia di Santa Cecilia. They also hosted the Opera season with a temporary, removable outdoor stage erected at some distance from the structures of the *caldarium*, so as to avoid damaging the Baths, which in a number of cases were actually preferred by directors as a unique, monumental stage set.

Aida at the Baths of Caracalla
(summer 2006)

2

The Building Site and Its Architecture

The Building Site and Its Architecture

The Baths of Caracalla occupy a rectangular area of approximately 337 × 328 meters. The construction of the site was a great feat of engineering. In order to create the platform and camber the different levels between the small Aventine hill and the Camene Valley, a site made of three large sloping terraces was developed, the northernmost side of which was constructed using brick arches which, at the same time, formed the substructure of the platform and the underground levels utilized for facilities. The opposite side was, instead, enclosed by the surrounding wall that supported and contained the hill which was quarried for material used in the construction of the Baths. The difference in elevation between the upper and lower level was about 14 meters, but the first level was partially filled with compacted dirt till it reached the walking level of 26 meters above sea level. In the lower level, all the service galleries, underground passages and sewers, as well as storing areas, were found.

It has been calculated that, for the construction of the building, 9000 workers were employed daily for approximately five years. This number included those who quarried or produced the materials and transported them to the site, those who participated in the construction and finally those who decorated it. The bricks alone, both in the underground and above ground areas, numbered several million. There were at least 252 columns, sixteen of which were more than 12 meters high.

The water supply was guaranteed by the aqueduct, *aqua Nova Antoniniana*, that took its name after the Emperor who

Octagonal Hall of the eastern surrounding wall, commonly known as the Temple of Jupiter

commissioned the work. Its waters derived from the *aqua Marcia* aqueduct, amplified by the tapping of new springs. The construction of the aqueduct must have been a pivotal moment during the planning of the Baths. It is possible to date its construction to the year AD 212 (the second year in which Caracalla reigned alone) from the dedication inscription of the new canal. The route of the aqueduct is not traceable with any degree of certainty except for one section already known for years that passes from the gate known as the Arch of Drusus (an overpass of the aqueduct on the Walls of Aurelian) in front of Porta Appia, to the Baths. Other small sections have also been definitely identified: a 5-meter long segment was found at the height of the Circonvallazione Appia, another 4.5 meters long was identified in Piazza Galeria and yet another was found at the intersection of the Walls of Aurelian. The underground aqueducts are much less recognizable. Beyond the Arch of Drusus, a 6-meter-long segment has been preserved at Largo delle Terme di Caracalla. Many arcades of the aqueduct are still visible in

The front of the cisterns

a section along Viale Guido Baccelli, even though partially covered by vegetation. The aqueduct (*castellum aquae*) arrived on the southern side of the Baths, and emptied eighteen (partially conserved) cisterns which guaranteed an augmented supply of water when needed for maintenance (emptying the pools, replacing lead piping, cleaning the rooms before and after bathing hours, etc.).

Recent studies on the hydraulic system of the Baths have revealed the complexity of the project and operation of the supply, systems of heating, and drainage. As we have already said, the supply of water was guaranteed by the Antoninianus aqueduct. From the cisterns, lead pipes branched off and under pressure supplied water to all of the areas of the building, with various routes and branch lines, which reached all the pools and fountains spread throughout the Baths. The pools of the *frigidarium* and *natatio* were probably fed continually, while the hot water pools were most likely filled and emptied from time to time. The sewer system was developed around a large central gallery, about 10 meters

One of the furnaces for heating the baths of the *caldarium* kept in the underground chamber

☛ The Passageways

In the planimetric layout of the Baths of Caracalla, the thermal areas were placed on a single axis while the dressing rooms and *palaestrae* were doubled and symmetrical. This permitted a greater flux of bathers, allowing them to constantly come and go freely, through ring and conjunctive routes on the longitudinal axis. In the smaller sized baths and private ones, bathers were forced to walk through longer, sometimes tortuous pathways, and often had to retrace their footsteps.

From the main entrances on the northern side, which led directly into the *natatio* (N), bathers could go directly into the *apodyteria* (M) to leave their clothes. From there, they then could return to the *natatio*, and, during summer, go directly into the outside pool, otherwise go exercise in the *palaestrae* (L). In the northern side of the *palaestrae*, there were three big rooms, onto which more entrances of the building opened. These rooms had colored mosaic floors, some of which still show the damage from the collapse of the immense vaults which supported the second floor. After exercising, the visitors would probably go back to the *natatio* or to the *frigidarium* (O); otherwise, walk around and go into the garden (B). From there, they could have entered any of the four areas situated on the sides of the caldarium (G), which we suppose were for *sudationes,* because of the

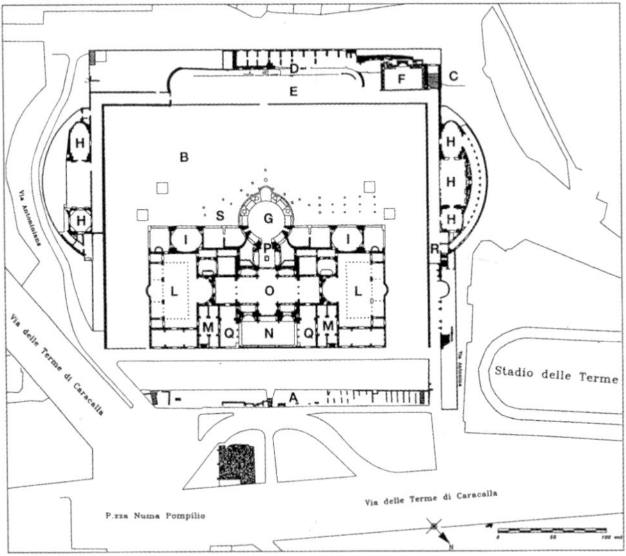

The plan of the complex with details of the main rooms

A = *Tabernae* of surrounding wall
B = Garden or *Xystus*
C = Stairway
D = Cisterns
E = Stadium (?)
F = Library
G = *Caldarium*
H = Hall
I = *Laconicum*
L = *Palaestra*
M = *Apodyterium*
N = *Natatio*
O = *Frigidarium*
P = *Tepidarium*
Q = *Vestibulum*
R = *Mythraeum*
S = The underground levels

presence of connecting cavities for hot air. The *sudationes* prepared the body for the hot baths that were to follow in the *caldarium*. According to the reconstruction of Blouet, the wall of the *laconica* (I) had a large opening facing the garden, interposed by columns surmounted by an architrave and by a wide arched window. If there existed windows, and the walls were not solid, then the windows probably had glass that would have stopped the dispersion of heat and simultaneously enhance solar insulation, given the eastern-western exposure. From the *caldarium*, bathers would pass to the *tepidarium* (P) and from there into the large indoor area, the *frigidarium*, which was the fulcrum of the building. From there, it was possible to reach the various rooms of the building.

below the floor level of the Baths, into which sewage and rain water would flow. The proper functioning of the underground maintenance system was guaranteed by the massive network of galleries that served every part of the Baths. Underneath the *caldarium* in the underground level, was placed the entire heating system with the *praefurnia* (there must have been about fifty *prafurniae,* although only twenty-four are preserved today, but others can be hypothesized from the traces left on the brickwork and by the symmetrical layout of the complex) and the cauldrons (or boilers) for heating water. The furnaces burned an average of ten tons of wood a day. The wood was stored in specific parts of the galleries used as warehouses. It has been calculated that the underground level could store more than 2000 tons of wood, enough to operate the *thermae* for a period of seven months.

Another pivotal moment in the construction of the Baths, in addition to the installation of the aqueduct, must have been the creation of the new road leading to the Baths, the *via Nova Antoniniana,* which ran in front of the northern side of the complex, connecting the *Circus Maximus* to *via Appia.* Ancient authors refer to its beauty and width and it was surely a worthy access to what must have been the most beautiful Baths of the city, one of the buildings richest in artwork. The *via Nova Antoniniana* was wide enough to transport building materials that, brought in large quantities, had to be warehoused at the Baths. While there were probably four roads leading to the main side of the building (the northern part), only one entry, on the southwestern side, is visible today. This entrance had a large monumental stairway on the side of the small Aventine hill.

The planimetric outline of the Baths is that of the "great imperial baths." Not only was the complex used for bathing, but also for strolling, studying, exercising and caring for the body. The central thermal building itself was oriented to the northeast/southwest. It was completely separated from

A panorama of the Baths

the surrounding walls, where there could be found the cisterns (D) and the two symmetrical libraries (F) to the south, two large *exedras* (H) enclosing warm areas and meeting places to the east and west, and main roads and *tabernae* to the north (A). On the southern side, in front of the cisterns was a stairway, which it is reasonable to believe was not part of a stadium, according to the general identification, but rather part of a waterfall. On the southwestern corner of the complex, a monumental stairway (C) represented the access to the Baths from the Aventine Hill. Next to this structure, and still distinguishable, are the remains of one of the two libraries of the wall. It was subject to many excavations in the eighties, after those carried out in 1912 that led to its discovery. The room has a rectangular shape of 38 × 22 meters and it has three walls covered by niches, thirty-two in all. Each niche served to contain the wooden *armaria* to store the books. Instead, in a larger niche in the center of the southern wall, the statue of *Athena* or another sculptural

The southeast library with niches
for the volumes

group must have been placed. In front of the three walls, the Romans built a masonry ledge that is believed to have served as a long bench for consulting the *volumina* (scripts). The marble floor of the library is a beautiful example of *opus sectile* intarsio with square and rectangular patterns and inscribed discs. Many of the multicolored marble fragments can still be found today at the site.

The outer wall of the Baths, surrounded by arcades, was separated from the central body by means of a large *xystus*, or garden, (B) where bathers could walk around and converse. According to Vitruvius and Plinius, it was the favorite garden close to the more sumptuous villas and palazzos, and it had arcades surrounding it on one or more sides.

The layout of the central building is presented as a closed rectangular area of about 214 × 110 meters, from which only the circular *caldarium* (G) and two small lateral *exedrae* protrude. The *exedrae* are encompassed in two symmetrically arranged rectangular areas that are identified, even by con-

The northeast *palaestra*

fronting its planimetry, to other thermal buildings, as the *palaestrae* (L) surrounded by arcades and possibly covered in the central part. Other areas were clearly marked for their specific uses: the *apodyteria*, or dressing room (M); the *natatio* (N), or outside pool; the *frigidarium*, a large covered area with four cold water pools on the longer sides (O); the *tepidarium* (P), which had two pools; and the *caldarium* (G), which had seven pools set up for hot water bathing. On the sides of the *caldarium* are situated the *laconica* (saunas) for *sudationes* (I). The building consisted of two floors at least in the *palaestrae* and the rooms connected to them and the *apodyteria* in two of which are still preserved the entry stair-

The eastern *apodyterium*

way illuminated by small windows leading to the second floor. Although it is difficult to identify the use of the rooms on the second floor, we believe that they were used for massages, heliotherapy and depilation.

Studying the prints of the building in greater detail, other areas are apparent: the *vestibula* (Q), the entrances on the northern side, the *apodyteria* and the *palaestrae*, which were doubled and symmetrical with respect to the actual central thermal body; the *natatio*, *frigidarium*, *tepidarium* and *caldarium* were instead located within the central body along one axis, to minimize the heat loss and, at the same time, maximize insolation and exposure from the hottest side to the west, where the summer sun would hit till dusk.

A room of real architectural and monumental importance is the *frigidarium*, a large hall that was the actual center of the main body of the Baths. It was located between the *natatio* and the *caldarium* and, with the latter constituted the most remarkable part of the thermal complex. The *frigidarium* was a large hall, 58 × 24 meters, covered by three cross-

A top view of the western *apodyterium*

vaults that rested on eight colossal columns made of grey Egyptian granite. The columns were placed against the walls that actually supported the axial thrust and at the same time articulated the transition to the adjacent areas. On the northern side, the elevation had three large arches that framed the beautiful niched walls of the *natatio*.

All the columns were interconnected by two rows of arcades, the higher one of which had large windows. Within four large niches, at the extremities of the long walls, were placed pools of cold water. These pools were dominated by large arches and opened onto the great hall with two columns of porphyry.

The large hall had marble floors with *opus sectile* intarsio. The floors were made of large marble slabs with granite and porphyry set within squares. The walls were covered by a polychrome marble plinth, of which only the underlying material remains. Probably, the niches in the walls where the statues were placed had a mosaic facing of vitreous paste, which created an iridescent effect with water. Primarily, the *frigidarium* served as a meeting point for the visitors of the baths who would then sort to one room or another of the thermal complex. Its central position made it the fulcrum for

The northern side of the *frigidarium*

the movements of the bathers. At the same time, the *frigidarium* had the function of containing the covered cold baths, with four large pools, two of which communicated with the *tepidarium* on the southern side and the other two instead, connected with the *natatio*, on the northern side, through a play of waterfalls. On this side, there are indications on the floor of a large circular fountain pool in between two large brick pools. This fountain pool has been preserved at the Archeological Museum of Naples. The *frigidarium* was a

The *frigidarium* in a famous reconstruction by Viollet Le Duc (1867)

monumental hall similar to a Basilica. It has inspired the architecture of many subsequent public buildings, such as the Baths of Diocletian and the Basilica of Massenzio, but its influence did not stop with imperial buildings. In fact, the architects who built, in the 1800s, the Chicago Railroad Station and Pennsylvania Station in New York copied its architecture perfectly.

The *caldarium* was another room of great monumental and architectural importance. It had a circular outline with marble floors and was covered by a *cupola* (dome) of almost 36 meters in diameter, only slightly smaller than that of the Pantheon. The walls had a double series of arches along them, which transferred the weight of the *cupola* onto only eight pillars of masonry; under the arches there were large windows of glass that must have contributed notably to the solar heating of the area and at the same time reduced the weight of the entire structure. The *caldarium* connected with the *tepidarium* through a small passage and with the saunas (*laconica*) through two side doors. Under this area,

The *laconica*, western side

there were furnaces to heat the water for the seven marble pools which measured 9 × 5 meters × 1 meter each. Of the seven, only six remain. The seventh pool was replaced by a small apse placed on the southern side during the mentioned restoration of Constantine. A passage from the *Historia Augusta* concerning a *cellam solearem* in a daring bronze structure has created much controversy regarding the identification of this area within the complex. Today we can definitely identify the *caldarium* (or *cella soliaris* from the Latin *solium* = tub) with a metal vault under the cupola.

Even the *natatio*, which contained a true Olympic size swimming pool, must have been a room of great monumental impact. Its northern façade was divided into three parts by gigantic grey granite columns. Each part had six niches for statues of two separate levels, three for each of the two levels, the lower one made of *Caristio* marble and the higher, made of *Granito del Foro* (a medium grain, predominantly white granite spackled uniformly with black, from the Mons Claudianus in Egypt, so named because of the large quantities found by Roman marble workers in Trajan's Forum). In the row of niches on the bottom floor, the plumbing that led into the pool with a waterfall is still visible. The area was of grandiose dimensions, 50 × 22 meters. The walls were over 20 meters in height. Bathers entered the pool from a stairway on the short sides of the wall. The pool was not very deep and thus it was inappropriate for diving. A comparison of styles can be made with the *frontes scenae* (stages) of the Hellenistic theaters, but most of all with the both geographically and chronologically closer *Septizodium*, built by the father of Caracalla, Septimius Severus.

Next pages
View of the *natatio*

3

The *Mythraeum* and the Underground Levels

The *Mythraeum* and the Underground Levels

The least known part of the Baths of Caracalla is the system of underground passages used for maintenance, which consisted in a maze of large and carriageable galleries (6 meters in height and 6 meters in width) that ran under most of the building. The storage rooms for wood, the water mill, the *Mythraeum,* the heating system, the furnaces, the cauldrons and the plumbing system were all in the underground level. The plumbing system was a massive network of small galleries that was used to lay lead piping and manage the intake and distribution of water. It must have been perfectly organized to permit maintenance crews to perform the necessary requirements for the correct functioning of such a large thermal complex and one with so many visitors. In fact, as we have already mentioned, calculating the dimensions of the pools and the rooms and the average time a visitor would spend in the *palaestra*, in the saunas and in the hot and cold baths, the Baths of Caracalla could have easily accommodated some 6000 to 8000 people each day.

The largest galleries were those used for the heating system, which ran for hundreds of meters under the building. They were lit by skylight windows that permitted a flow of air and inhibited the wood stored there from rotting. The large dimensions of the galleries derived from the necessity to bring in wagons full of wood and pulled by horses. Troughs for the horses were positioned in three niches lined with fragments of pottery placed in one of the walls of the three symmetrical galleries, on the western side. The barrel vaults covering the underground ceiling were lined with

End wall of the *Mythraeum*.
In the middle the relief
with the *petra genetrix*

square bricks (*bessales*) measuring 19 × 19 centimeters which were in turn lined with *bipedali* (two-foot square bricks). It is the intention of the Archeological Superintendent of Rome to restore and open to the public at least part of the fascinating underground passages, which contribute significantly to the comprehension of the mechanical functioning of the thermal complex.

The excavation of the water mill began in 1912. It was originally erroneously dated to late antiquity or Middle Ages. Only recently two Swedish scholars, Schiøler and Wikander, have correctly reconstructed its use. They convincingly dated it by the building techniques, which matched those of the rest of the complex, and by some fragments of ceramic found in the site which dated to the construction of the Baths. It is possible that the water mill was an original installation and necessary for the functioning of the thermal complex, in consideration of the large number of bathers that passed through and their numerous requirements.

The water mill was probably burnt in the second half of the third century and it was rebuilt with some variations in the layout. Surely it was active at least till the fifth century, a period when the Baths were perfectly functional, as ancient authors (Polemius Silvius and Olympiodorus) testify and as data from recent excavations confirm.

The *Mythraeum* was unearthed on occasion of the large excavations done in the area at the beginning of the 1900s, and the details were published by its discoverer, Ettore Ghislanzoni. Access to the *Mythraeum* and the galleries was possible through an entrance on *via Antoniniana*. The galleries were separated from the *Mythraeum* by a door or a gate.

There were five areas: the first was a sort of entrance and the space under the stairway which led to the floor of the Baths; this area had a small semicircular pool, on the short northern end, which was covered by a semicupola lined with ceramic fragments. From here, crossing a travertine threshold (one of the many preserved in the *Mythraeum*) and a passageway, one entered into another area, separated by a gate or door, where, in the 1912, was found the statue of *Aphrodite Anadiomene* now displayed in the ex Planetarium. Hence, there was the entrance to the real *Mythraeum*, the largest in Rome, consisting of a large rectangular room, covered with a crossed vaulted ceiling. The floor was covered with a black and white mosaic with benches on the long side of the walls. At the entrance to the room a circular pit, dug into the floor, is visible. It was covered by a flat marble slab in which a large terracotta containing staves of wheat

A view of the *Mythraeum* with
the *fossa sanguinis* in the center

was partially buried. A fresco representing Mythra or a torch bearer, with a Fregian head-covering and with a solar disc on its belly, is still recognizable on the long western wall. The room was devoid of any other decoration except for a marble block, roughly carved (called *petra genetrix*), representing a snake in the rocks from which the god was born. The most important element was a hole, made of brick, in the center of the room. It was connected by way of a narrow passageway and a stairway to another adjacent room, that opened onto what we can consider a "sacristy" (or a kitchen?). This room had a large, roughly-made counter with a curtain wall of brick in the back and a small circular pool with steps that must have served for the ablutions connected with the sacrifice.

On the use of the rectangular hole, an *unicum* among the known *Mythraea*, the interpretations are different. A majority

Fresco with Mythra in the niche
in the west wall

of scholars including the author of this book believes that it must be a *fossa sanguinis* (hole of blood) for the sacrifice of a bull (*taurobolium*) that was killed on an iron grate placed on top of the hole, where the person initiated, dressed in a white toga, was ready to be covered by the bull's blood. Others believe it was a trap door for a "spectacular apparition." The first theory seems more plausible in that it connects better to the religious beliefs of Caracalla and his family, directed towards religious syncretism that almost blended classical and oriental gods into one single cult and that unified, within the same building of cult, already in an imperial bath, a statue of Aphrodite, an inscription dedicated to Serapi *Kosmokrator*, to which the name of the Egyptian god was erased and substituted with Mythra's name, and, finally, the hole for the *taurobolium*, connected to the cult of Mythra but also to that of Attis.

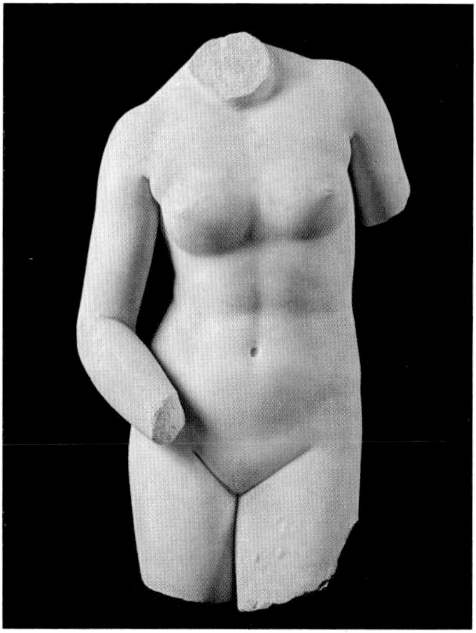

Statue of the Aphrodite Anadyomene from the *Mythraeum* (excavation of 1912). Rome, Museo Nazionale Romano, octagonal hall of the Baths of Diocletian

4

The Decorations and Works of Art

The Decorations and Works of Art

The Baths of Caracalla, although known as the "villas of the plebeians" because of their location in the working class section of Rome, at the *regio Aventina* near the commercial area of the Testaccio, were, according to ancient authors, "eximias et magnificentissimas." Their lavish decoration included floors made from oriental colored marbles and glass-paste mosaics and marbles on the walls, stucco paintings and hundreds of statues in the niches of the rooms, and in the most important halls and gardens. Some of the statues were made of bronze, while most of them were painted marble and must have caught the eye in the richly polychrome baths.

Of all the Roman bath complexes, the Baths of Caracalla have yielded up the most sculptural remains, even though many of its statues ended up in the lime kilns of the Middle Ages. The first systematic collection of its sculptures was carried out by Pope Paul III Farnese, between 1545 and 1547, during the excavations at the Antoniana to decorate his new palazzo. The discovery of the Farnese bull, probably in the eastern *palaestra,* created much excitement among contemporaries. The famous colossal marble group was sculpted out of a solid block of marble and represents the torture of Dirce who was tied to a bull by Amphion and Zethus to vindicate the mistreatment done unto their mother, Antiope, who looks on. Because of its colossal size, the group was placed in the courtyard of the Farnese Palazzo, facing Via Giulia. It is not clear whether the sculpture was adapted and transformed (possibly into a fountain) right at the time of its discovery. The Farnese bull was so famous that King Louis

The west *palaestra*. In the foreground, the celebrated polychrome mosaics

XIV of France tried unsuccessfully to buy it and take it to Paris. It was not its destiny, however, to remain in Rome. It was transported to Naples in 1788, along with a large portion of the Farnese collection and given in dowry to the last member of the Farnese family, Elisabeth. She married the King of Spain, Philip V, and subsequently the statue was given to her son, Charles of Bourbon, King of Naples. At first it was put on public display at the Villa Reale of Chiaia and subsequently in 1826 it was transferred to the National Archeological Museum of Naples. It can still be found there along with many other masterpieces from the Baths. Another statue worth mentioning is the famous colossal Farnese Hercules found in the *frigidarium*. It had been signed on its base by

Figurated capital with Hercules from the *frigidarium*, preserved in the underground level

Farnese Hercules found
in the *frigidarium*. Naples,
Museo Nazionale Archeologico

Glykon, an Athenian sculptor working at the beginning of the third century AD. Pietro Santi Bartoli (Flaminio Vacca, *Memorie,* 77) narrates that the body was found in the Baths, the head at the bottom of a pit in Trastevere and the legs in Frattocchie. The notoriety of this statue was so great that it was replicated in every size, from that of the actual statue of 3 meters, to terracotta copies of only a few centimeters. Another big size statue, the so-called Latin Hercules, was found in the *frigidarium* of the Baths of Caracalla. At first, it was given up for lost but then identified in the large statue preserved at the Reggia di Caserta. Hercules was loved by the Severus family and therefore frequently portrayed in the Baths, where one of the most famous figural capitals of antiquity was found in the *frigidarium:* the semi-god represented in a resting position, leaning on his club.

Other sculptures have been found at different times in the Baths—the statues of Atreus and Thyestes, the statue of Minerva, of Venus and busts representing the important mem-

One of the two fountains made with the big granite pools of the *frigidarium*. Rome, Piazza Farnese

bers of the imperial family. Numerous architectonic fragments were also found, among which the pools, which are now in the Belvedere courtyard in the Vatican, and two beautiful pools of grey granite, found in the *frigidarium,* were reutilized as fountains by Rainaldi in Piazza Farnese. Also noteworthy is the granite column found in the *natatio* which was brought to Florence and raised, by Cosimo I de' Medici, in Piazza Santa Trinità, where it still stands.

The statues in the niches must have been an eye-catching part of the decorations. They were placed in most of the walls and in almost all of the rooms except for the hottest ones. The statues have been calculated to have numbered more than 120, a large portion of which is scattered in museum collections throughout Europe. This confirms the news given to us by Pietro Santi Bartoli (Flaminio Vacca, *Memorie*, 78) that there were so many digs at the Baths of Caracalla that they filled entire warehouses of the Farnese Palace even though many beautiful fragments were recycled into lime, as was the habit of the time! Surely the statue of Artemis found in the underground levels in 1996 must have been initially placed in a niche, since its drapery is accurately and highly carved in the front while in contrast the back is barely worked. Therefore, it must have been destined only for a frontal view.

Of all the sculptural architectonic decoration of the Baths, about 2000 fragments still exist in the warehouses. Among them are the famous colossal figural capitals from the *frigidarium*, portraying eagles and lightning bolts, fragments of decorations with arms from the *palaestrae*, bases, columns and frames. The quality of the marbles was countless. White Greek marble, mostly Proconnesian but also Parian, Tasian, *pavonazzetto* and Lunensis, grey and red granite, porphyry, serpentine, antique yellow, white marble veined with purple, *cipollino* and other varieties were also used.

Finally, the mosaics and marble floors are also worth remembering. In fact, the floors are among the most complete and decorative elements in Rome, where it is difficult to find a repertoire so ample and chronologically homogeneous. The floors of the central body (*frigidarium*, *tepidarium* and *caldarium*) were all done in marble with *opus sectile* intarsio, of which we have no remains except for a few fragments in the *caldarium* and *frigidarium*. The *palaestrae* floors and those of the rooms connected to them and the vestibules of the *natatio* had colored marble mosaic tesseras with large use of crushed serpentine stone and antique yellow. They had extremely varied and original motifs portraying the flavor and the notable richness of inventiveness of the time.

Those of the *apodyteria*, instead, had simple white and black mosaics with geometric designs different one from the other. Moreover, the mosaics of the *palaestrae* were of colored marbles with curvilinear motifs and a beautiful volute

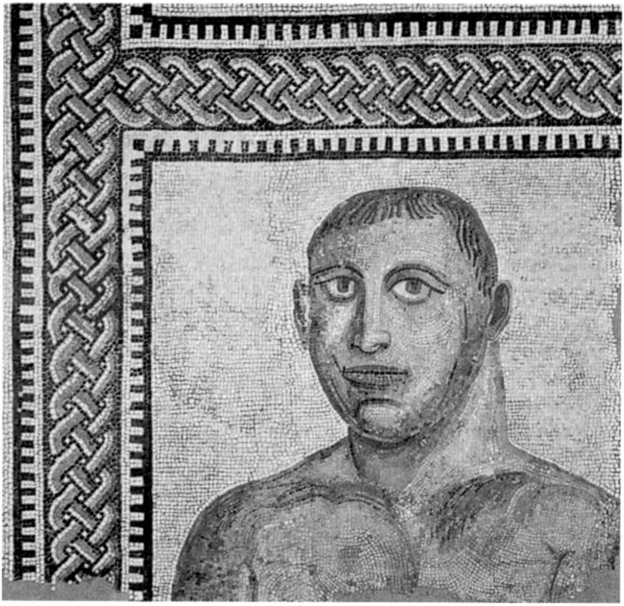

Fragment of the mosaic with athletes, located in the exedra of the *palaestrae*. Rome, Museo Nazionale Romano, Palazzo Massimo alle Terme

motif in the center made with serpentine rock. In the two apses, in the 1824 excavations, the famous mosaics of athletes were found. In 1838, they were transferred to the Museum of the Lateran Palace. In 1963, they were transferred to the Vatican Museums where in the 1970s they were remounted to their original order and primitive semicircular form.

Probably, at the time of the removal of the mosaics from the exedra of the *palaestra*, a few detailed watercolors were made to document its state before the removal.

The floors were boarded by a black trim and were divided internally into rectangular, square and irregularly shaped panels: the first contained life-size portraits of athletes or judges, the second representations of larger than life-size busts of athletes and the third representations of the equipment and prizes for the athletes. The athletes are immediate-

Mosaic with a marine *thiasos* from the upper floor of the *palaestrae*

Next page
The mosaics from the *palaestrae*

ly distinguished from the judges by their nudity, and according to their attributes, we can distinguish the winners, with a palm branch and crown, boxers, discus throwers, javelin throwers, and wrestlers. The judges of the games wear long tunics, have short hair and beards, and hold a palm branch used as a signaling device. The equipment represented in the other spaces includes bars and palm branches.

The floors on the upper levels above the *palaestrae* were decorated with thiasus marine motifs with Nereids, tritons and dolphins, cupids and marine monsters. It was about 300 meters long. It collapsed from the upper floors and now lies in large fragments leaning against the walls of the two *palaestrae* and in other areas of the central body.

The walls of the Baths were decorated with marble slabs (*crustae*), recognizable by small holes for the nails which were used to support them and which allow us to reconstruct the rectangular design. The vaults facing the *natatio* and the niches of the pools of the *frigidarium* were, instead, probably covered by mosaics made with vitreous paste which must have created an iridescent effect as it reflected the pool of water.

The mosaic with a marine *thiasos* belonging to the terrace of the western *palaestra*

A fragment of the mosaic with a marine *thiasos* motif located on the terrace of the eastern *palaestra*: bull or sea monster

5

Caracalla

Caracalla

Marcus Aurelius Antoninus Bassianus was born in Lugdunum on April 4, AD 188, when his father Septimius Severus was governor of the Gaelic province. Septimius Severus, an ambitious senator of African origin, was acclaimed as emperor by the legions of the Danube in AD 193 and remained sole commander of the empire in 197 after he freed himself of all the other claimants. Iulia Domna, the mother of Caracalla, was the daughter of the high priest of El Gabal at Emesa. Her horoscopes predicted that she would marry a king. Caracalla had a brother, Geta. Since childhood, sibling rivalry existed between the two. Sources describe him as an amiable and intelligent child always ready to perform acts of kindness "sed haec puer," but this was his childhood. When he turned fifteen in AD 203, his father, Septimius Severus, who had become emperor two years earlier, made him marry Plautilla, daughter of his favorite, Plautianus. Five years later he brought Caracalla with him in Britannia. There Bassianus had already deeply changed his character, becoming more grim and stern and obsessed by the desire to resemble Alexander the Great. He took part in the war against the Caledonians with his father and his brother Geta. In February AD 211 Septimius Severus died in Eboracum and his sons rushed to conclude a peace agreement and return to Rome at the beginning of May with their mother Iulia Domna to rule together. Herodian narrated of how the imperial palace on the Palatine hill was divided in half, with separate entrances and vestibules, so that the brothers would not meet. Even the empire was divided into

Portrait of Caracalla.
Rome, Museo Nazionale Romano,
Palazzo Massimo alle Terme

two. Caracalla kept the western part. In February AD 212 Geta died in his mother's arms killed by his brother.

Ancient authors write that after the murder, Caracalla, although he escaped a murder plot himself ordered by Geta, found refuge with the army. Subsequently, he convinced the praetorians, with many gifts and promises, to proclaim him sole emperor, after which he made the friends and partisans of Geta disappear. More than a thousand victims died this way. Among them was the famous jurist Papinianus, a great friend of his father, to whom Caracalla turned for defense against the accusation of fratricide. The jurist disdainfully refused, saying that forgiving a fratricide was not as easy as committing it. Caracalla therefore abandoned himself to a series of acts of bloodshed alternated by periods of pathological religiousness. During one of these episodes he deified his brother, while, beforehand, he ordered the *damnatio memoriae,* meaning the disappearance of any effigy or written record of Geta. Caracalla would write to the Senate that the spirit of Alexander the Great lived in him. In fact, he started walking with his head tilted towards the right, as in the famous depictions of Alexander the Great. Caracalla granted the management of the internal politics to the *consilium principis*, presided by his mother who was, to all effects, the reigning empress and responsible for the empire. Caracalla, on the other hand, occupied himself with his beloved army. Iulia Domna reigned as an uncontested empress mother. She had direction and control of administrative problems, of the registries and of the imperial Greek and Latin correspondence. Her titles *Pia* and *Felix,* reserved till that time only for emperors, guaranteed her place and legitimized her in name of the imperial *pietas* and Augustan charisma. She governed the Roman world as mother of the empire. She probably did not love her fratricidal son but knew he would reign a long time supported unconditionally by the army. While in practice his mother ruled the empire, Caracalla is credited for many military accomplishments in

Europe and the Orient, both in defending the boundaries from invaders and finding new economical sources of revenue. During the spring and summer of AD 213, he left for Gaul where, at Narbona, he killed many citizens and the Governor of the province. It is probably from this area that he imported the cloak, called Caracalla, from which he was nicknamed. It had a wide hood which he loved to wear and he had it distributed to the Roman citizens. Then he left for Germany to wage war against the Chatti and Alemanni but he was defeated and had to buy peace at a high price. The following year he went to Thrace to fight against the Getae. From there he continued on to Asia minor and found a colony at Edessa. Having heard that the inhabitants of

Portrait of Septimius Severus.
Rome, Museo Nazionale Romano,
Palazzo Massimo alle Terme

Alexandria spoke of him with contempt and disapproved of his fratricide, he ransacked and pillaged the city. Finally in AD 215 he went to Antioch to prepare war against the Parthians. He plundered the area, dispersed the kings' bones and ransacked the sepulchres. From there he went back to Edessa to spend the winter (216–217) and he celebrated the Parthian victory by printing coins. In 217, while traveling to visit the temple of the god Lunes between Edessa and Carrhae, a soldier stabbed him while coming down from his horse by order of Macrinus, Caracalla's own prefect, who had himself proclaimed emperor by the soldiers. In synthesis, this is the biography of Caracalla according to Dion Cassius and the *Historia Augusta*, but Caracalla's life and accomplishments should also be analyzed on the basis of indisputable historic information. If the ancient authors were not very generous with the emperor, describing him as insane, bloodthirsty and fratricidal, history must give him credit for his extraordinary accomplishments in furthering the evolution of the empire. In fact, Caracalla's politics consisted of

Portrait of Iulia Domna.
Rome, Museo Nazionale Romano,
Palazzo Massimo alle Terme

achieving internal unification by placing all citizens on a same standard. Consequence and instrument of this political design was the extension of Roman citizenship to all the inhabitants of the provinces, the *Constitutio Antoniniana*. The empire, moreover, was going through a serious political and economic crisis. The very large amount of remuneration being freely given to the army required a constant influx of money, procured partially by doubling the inheritance taxes and fines, as well as with new monetary provisions which reduced the value of money. At that time a new function, the *Corrector Italiae*, was instituted with the task to reorganize the finances of the Italian municipalities.

The *Constitutio Antoniniana* is hardly remembered by the historians. Dion Cassius, a principal figure and direct witness to these years, speaks of this only in a passage which describes the oppressive tormenting measures, which Caracalla used to increase state revenue and enrich his beloved soldiers. Herodian, another author of almost the same age of Caracalla and an imperial officer, does not speak of this at all. Neither does the *Historia Augusta*, which reports even minute references of the emperor. The indifference or lack of comprehension of the importance of the edict should not surprise us, because very often the great transformations of history are not understood by the contemporaries, but only by the descendants. In fact, with the *Constitutio Antoniniana*, the empire became a common homeland to all the inhabitants residing in it, who could identify themselves with the title *civis Romanus*, and were citizens subject to the same laws in any part of the empire. Another measure adopted by Caracalla was the printing of the *Antoninianus*, a coin having the same amount of silver in it as the *denarius*, but worth one and a half times its value. The *Antoninianus* was destined to become, during the third century, the main coin of the system. This was an ingenious solution, whereby the money was not devaluated by decreasing the percentage of noble metal, but rather by decreasing its standard weight. It was a directive that tended to stabilize the monetary system with the coining of a nominal silverpiece that was less overvalued than the *denarius* with respect to its fine metal content. In reality it seems that the monetary reform of Caracalla, subject to different interpretations by historians, must have been caused by the need to reestablish trust in the imperial coin, which was strongly weakened after the drastic devaluation made by Septimius Severus, father of Caracalla. This directive, however, was not enough to resolve the inflationary crisis of the State. The general expenditures had grown significantly with the number of legions needed by Septimius Severus, but the persistence of danger on the Rhine, Danube and on the eastern fronts, made it impossible to curb military expenditures. If the literary tradition, near to the Senate, has always depicted Caracalla as an emperor that generously spent for his army, it is also true that the imperial power, in this way, was aware of the decisive role that the army played, even greater than in the past.

The expenditures for the military could not be cut and, moreover, the tributes were urging to buy peace with the barbarians. Furthermore, expenses for public works and those for the food supply for the capital increased. In fact, distributions for the Roman citizens increased: oil, wine and pork were distributed on a regular basis. In conclusion we must re-evaluate the persona of the "cursed" emperor, in light of his numerous historic merits, the last of which were the beautiful Baths of Caracalla, and in consideration of his short and tumultuous reign.

The *caldarium* and *tepidarium* of the Baths seen from the south enclosure

6

The Life in the Baths

The Life in the Baths

"Here, from every direction, I hear sounds of every kind: I live right above the public bath. Now imagine all sorts of sounds that can make us hate our ears: when the strongest men exercise and shake their hands while holding large lead balls, or exert themselves or pretend to, I hear their sighs, when they exhale, and their hisses and unpleasant respiration. When some lazy person is happily being oiled in the most common way, I hear the sound of the hand that hits his shoulders, different when the hand is open or closed. Now, if a ball player comes and starts counting points, it's the end. Now add a troublemaker, and a thief caught in the act, and to that a person who enjoys hearing himself in the pool. Add those who jump in the pools, splashing. Besides these, whose voices are, at least, all the same tone, think about the depilator that speaks with a hollow and acute voice so that it can easily be heard and he is quiet only when he rips the hair from under the arms, forcing another to scream instead of himself. Think about the different screams of people who sell drinks, and those who sell sausages and pastries, and all the tavern owners who recommend their own products with a particular tone of voice." This passage is from the famous letter of Seneca to Lucilius from Baiae (*Epistles*, 56, 1–2). Still today it is the most vivacious representation of life in the Roman baths and if by chance it refers to small baths in a provincial peasant town, one can imagine what confusion there must have been in the larger, more frequented, baths like those of Caracalla. The words of Seneca, along with the celebrated epitaph on a Roman tomb of the imperial age

Detail of the *xystus*, restored by Rodolfo Lanciani in 1917

Lawrence Alma-Tadema, *A Favourite Custom* (1901). London, Tate Gallery

which reads: “The baths, the wines and Venus corrupt our bodies, but the baths, the wines and Venus are life,” give testimony of the importance that the baths had in the lives of the citizens. But it wasn’t always this way. During the Republican era, in fact, the bath was considered a Greek weakness. Both the patricians and slaves were advised to use them for as little time as possible, in order not to lose physical strength. The bath (*lavatrina*), in the richest houses, was located in a hidden corner of the house. Describing the bath of Scipio Africanus in his villa in Liternum, Seneca compares republican customs to the weaknesses of his time saying: ‘In that corner... he who was the terror of Carthage washed his tired body from the fatigue of the country under a filthy roof and on a very poor floor ... while in our times nobody would tolerate washing themselves like that, ... today the walls are shining with rare marbles from Egypt and Numidia, ... the vault is covered with very rich gilding ... and the Thasian marble, which at one time could only be admired in the rarest temples, today lines the pools where weak bodies, covered by sweat from the furnaces, dive into...” Around the second century BC, a few creative entrepreneurs opened public baths (*balnea*), sub-contracting them out so that, even by charging a small entrance fee, the *balneaticum*, they were able to make significant and fast gains.

The ritual of the baths traditionally consisted in a sauna, a hot bath, a cold bath and a massage. For men and women, they were held either in different rooms or at different hours. Later on, to the above, the performance of rigorous physical exercises, which included gymnastics, wrestling and playing ball, was added.

The oldest baths in ancient Italy are the Stabian Baths of Pompeii that date back to the fourth century BC and the very famous ones of Baiae, favored by the presence of hot mineral water springs and natural vapors around the volcanic area of Campi Flegrei. In Greece, the Baths of Olympia date back to the middle of the fifth century BC in their beginning phase.

In fact, it was an entrepreneur of Baiae, Sergius Orato, who, at the end of the second century BC, according to tradition, had the good idea to artificially reproduce the natural phenomenon of hot water and vapors, by inventing an artificial water heating system, which carried the water under the floors and along the walls of the thermal rooms. The word hypocaust defines the space under the floor where the wood-burning stove was lit. The heat of combustion traveled under the floor, which was held up by small pilasters (*suspensurae*), that remained warm while the heated water was simultaneously used for a hot bath in the pools (*solia* or *alvei*). This idea determined the success of the thermal system in all of the Roman world. In 33 BC there were 170 baths in Rome according to Agrippa's census. Agrippa, the son-in-law of Augustus, inaugurated the Baths ten years later, named after him in Campo Marzio, and gave free access to all Roman citizens. Its planimetric layout, however, still shows a casual placing of rooms around the central hall, typical of thermal buildings of the republican period. In the same district in AD 62, Nero built his beautiful baths, celebrated by Martial (VII, 34,4) "What is worse than Nero? What is better than his Baths?" This is the first bath where the thermal areas (*frigidarium, tepidarium, caldarium*) are situated on a long central axis, while the *palaestrae* and areas connected to them, are situated orthogonally to them. Titus inaugurated his baths in the Neronian area of *Domus Aurea*, but only very few remains and some drawings from the Renaissance survived. In AD 110, to the northeast of the *Domus Aurea*, Trajan inaugurated luxurious baths which took his name and which encompassed part of Nero's palace. These baths provided the canonical model for the "large imperial baths." They were a place to bathe, but were also rich in arcades and gardens, libraries and roads. The actual thermal structures were in the central body, separated from the garden by reading rooms and meeting areas, that were placed against the high enclosing walls that separated the complex from the city. The complex was perfectly oriented from northeast to southwest to take advantage of natural insulation. This characteristic was adopted later on by other thermal buildings. A century later, the Romans witnessed the inauguration of a thermal complex that was the most sumptuous and grandiose ever built, the Baths of Caracalla. The Baths of Diocletian, inaugurated ninety years later, were larger than those of Caracalla but not more magnificent.

All the baths were used as meeting places and as places to pass free time, exercise, care for the body, eat, meet friends and acquaintances and as a place to pass the entire afternoon from the opening time (between noon and 2 p.m.) till closing time, at dusk.

They were frequented by all social levels, from the most humble to the richest. Even the emperors were eager to go there. Augustus and Vespasian played ball there. Suetonius narrates (*Vespasian*, 20) that Vespasian would spend long hours in it. Among the ball players some were considered idols by the crowd, such as Ursus, known from an inscription of the second century AD (*CIL* VI, 9797), which reads: "The masses loved me and loud screams resounded in the Baths of Trajan, in those of Agrippa and Titus, and many also in the Baths of Nero: believe me, it is me, come and celebrate me, oh ball players and adorn, friends, my statue with flowers, violets and roses." Obviously there were also parasites, as the one known by the epigram of Martial (XII, 82): "In the baths and nearby areas, it is not possible to push aside Menogenes, even if you use any expedient. He will pick up the ball, with either his left or right sweaty hand, and score in your favor. He will pick up the ball that fell in the dirt and bring it to you, even if he already took a bath and was wearing sandals. He will praise you and admire you in everything until, after you have put up with his thousand annoyances, you will ask him to eat with you." The baths were frequented by a multitude of people and also by thieves, *fures balnearii*, that took advantage of the confusion to enter the dressing rooms (*apodyteria*) and steal unguarded objects. So frequent was the thieving that the rich went to the baths with a slave who was left to watch over the owner's belongings. Many different penalties existed for different types of thievery, ranging from forced labor to working in the mines (*Digesto*, XLVII, 17).

Women loved to go to the baths. In fact, we know from Varro (*De lingua latina*, I, 1, 9, 68) that already in the second century BC there were baths that were strictly divided for the two sexes. But Cicero still lamented that the division between the sexes was not always respected (*De Officiis*, I, 35, 129) and the same habits of the "promiscuous" baths scandalized Plinius the Elder (*Naturalis Historia*, XXXIII, 153), while Martial accepted it as the mirror of the permissive society of his time (III, 51, 72; XI, 47, 75). The emperor Hadrian, to stop this scandal, decreed a rigid separation of the sexes by using separate rooms or different hours (*Historia Augusta, Hadrianus*, 18, 10). The same decree was adopt-

View of the Baths at dawn

ed by Marcus Aurelius (*Historia Augusta, Marcus*, 23, 8) and by Severus Alexander (*Historia Augusta, Severus Alexander*, 24, 2), in contrast to an opposite one of vice-ridden Heliogabalus.

In general, the opening hours of the baths, as already mentioned, were concentrated between noon and 2 p.m. with closing hours around till dusk, even though there is proof that, in Pompeii and Lusitania, the baths could also stay open at night. The entrance fee varied but surely it must have been a very low fee. Horatius (*Satires*, I, 3, 37) and Martial (*Epigrams*, 11, 52, M, 30, 4) speak of a *quadrans*, a forth of an *asse* (the coin at the time). For one and a half *asse* a loaf of bread and one liter of wine could be bought. At the time of Diocletian the entrance fee was of 2 *denarii* (the smallest denomination of the bronze series) which included the custody at the baths of one's clothes. On special occasions, and in certain baths, entrance was free, a technique used by politicians to conquer the good will of the people.

Bibliography

A. Blouet, *Restauration des Thermes d'Antonin Caracalla à Rome*, Paris 1828.

G. Secchi, *Il musaico antoniniano rappresentante la scuola degli atleti*, Rome 1843.

E Rosa, *Scoperte archeologiche*, Rome 1873, p. 83 ff.

S.A. Iwanoff, *Architektonische Studien, III: Aus den Tbermen des Caracalla, mit Erläuterungen von Ch. Hülsen*, Berlin 1898.

G. De Angelis, *Relazione dei lavori eseguiti dall'Ufficio nel quadriennio 1899–1902*, Rome 1903, pp. 108–14.

E. Ghislanzoni, *Scavi nelle Terme Antoniniane*, "Notizie degli Scavi di antichità 1912, pp. 305–25; in particular for the walking level pp. 305–17 for the underground pp. 317–25.

G. Ripostelli, *Terme di Caracalla*, Rome 1916.

D. Krencker, E. Krüger, *Die Trierer Kaiserthermen*, Augsburg 1929, pp. 269–79.

S.B. Platner, T. Ashby, *A Topographical Dictionary of Ancient Rome*, London 1929, pp. 520–24.

E. Brödner, *Untersuchungen an den Caracallathermen*, Berlin 1951.

E. Nash, *Bildlexicon zur Topographie des antiken Rom*, II, Tübingen 1961–62, p. 434.

G. Lugli, *Le Terme di Caracalla*, Rome 1975.

I. Iacopi, *L'Arco di Costantino e le Terme di Caracalla*, Rome 1977.

H. Manderscheid, *Die Skuloturenaussiattung der kaiserzeitlichen Thermenanlagen*, Berlin 1981, pp. 73–76, nos. 46–68.

W Heinz, *Römische Thermen: Badewesen und Badeluxus im römischen Reich*, Munich 1983, pp. 124–41.

M. Marvin, "Freestanding sculptures from the Baths of Caracalla," *American Journal of Archaeology*, 87, 1983, pp. 347–84.

T. Schiøler, O. Wikander, "A Roman Water-mill in the Baths of Caracalla," *Opuscola Romana*, 14, 1983, pp. 47–64.

C. Gasparri, *Sculture provenienti dalle Terme di Caracalla e Diocleziano*, RIA, 6–7, 1983–84, pp. 133–41.

M. G. Cecchini, "Terme di Caracalla: campagna di scavo 1982–1983 lungo il lato orientale," in *Roma*, II, Rome 1985, pp. 583–93.

G. Jenewein, "*Statuenfragmente aus den Coracallathermen*," *Römische Historische Mitteilungen*, 1985, pp. 13–49.

D. Kinney, "Spolia from the Baths of Caracalla in Sta. Maria in Trastevere," *The Art Bulletin*, 68, 1986, pp. 379–97.

M. Piranomonte, A. Capodiferro, "Le Terme di Caracalla un luogo per lo sport e il tempo libero," in *Lo sport nel mondo antico*, exhibition catalogue, 1987, pp. 109–19.

J. Delaine, *The cella solearis of the Baths of Caracalla: a Reappraisal*, BSR, 55, 1987, pp. 147–55.

H. Manderscheid, *Bibliographie zuin rdmischen Badewesen*, 1988, pp. 180–82.

J. Delaine, *Recent Research on Roman Baths*, JRA, 1, 1988, pp. 19, 21–22, 26–29.

G. Tedeschi Grisanti, *Dalle Terme di Caracalla capitelli reimpiegati nel Duomo di Pisa*, RendLinc, 1, 1990, op. 161–85.

I. Nielsen, *Thermae et Balnea: The Architecture and Cultural History of Roman Public Baths*, Aarhus 1990, pp. 3–57.

M.L. Conforto, I. Iacopi, *Le Terme di Caracalla*, in *Roma Antiqua II. Grandi edifici pubblici*, exhibition catalogue, Rome 1992, pp. 234–54.

G. Garbrecht, H. Manderscheid, "Etiam fonte novo antoniniano: l'acquedotto antoniniano alle Terme di Caracalla," *Archeologia Classica*, 14, 1992, pp. 193–233.

E Yegül, *Baths and Bathing in Classical Antiquity*, Cambridge (MA), 1992, pp. 146–62.

M. Piranomonte, *Le Terme di Caracalla* in *Architetture di Roma Antica* II, Milan 1993, pp. 30–45.

M. Piranomonte, A. Capodiferro, "Terme di Caracalla. Lo scavo della biblioteca sud-ovest," in *La ciutàt en el mon Romà*, Proceedings of the XIV ArchCl Congress, 1994, pp. 333–35.

G. Garbrecht, H. Manderscheid, "Die Wasserbewirischaftung römiscber Thermen," in *Mitteilungen aus dem Leichtweiss Institut für Wasserbau*, 118, 1994, A, pp. 93–130.

Lombardi, A. Corazza, *Le Terme di Caracalla*, Rome 1995.

M. Piranomonte, *ad vocem* "Mithra, spelunca (Thermae Antoninianae)," in *Lexicon Topographicum Urbis Romae*, III, pp. 267–68.

J. Delaine, *The Baths of Caracalla in Rome*, JRA, suppl. 25, 1997.

M. Piranomonte, *ad vocem*, "Thermae Antoninianae," in *Lexicon Topographicum Urbis Romae*, being printed.

G. Jenewein, *Die Architekturdekoration der Caracallathermen*, being printed.

Photograph Credits
Archivio fotografico della Soprintendenza speciale per i beni archeologici di Roma/Bruno Angeli: cover, 6, 46, 54–55
Archivio fotografico della Soprintendenza speciale per i beni archeologici di Roma/Luciano Mandato: 15
Archivio fotografico della Soprintendenza speciale per i beni archeologici di Roma/Leandro Lentini: 20, 21, 26, 34–35, 38, 53, 57
Archivio fotografico della Soprintendenza speciale per i beni archeologici di Roma/Gianfranco Gentile: 29, 48
Archivio fotografico della Soprintendenza speciale per i beni archeologici di Roma/Gianfranco Gentile and Marcello Martini: 56
Archivio fotografico della Soprintendenza speciale per i beni archeologici di Roma/Marina Piranomonte: 27, 32, 67, 70, 76
Archivio fotografico della Soprintendenza speciale per i beni archeologici di Roma/Eugenio Monti: 41, 42
Archivio fotografico della Soprintendenza speciale per i beni archeologici di Roma/Luciano Pedicini: 49
Archivio fotografico della Soprintendenza speciale per i beni archeologici di Roma: 52, 60, 63, 64
Mondadori Electa Archive, Milan: 72
Adriano La Regina: 24
Studio Vasari: 9, 10, 11, 12, 13, 18, 28, 30, 43, 50

This volume was printed by Mondadori Electa S.p.A., at Elcograf S.p.A., via Mondadori 15, Verona, in 2014